Definit

Eric was surprised when he saw the dolphin. He'd never seen one before, but all the same he knew what dolphins were. He also knew where you found them, and this was definitely *not* where.

Not in a ten-foot-wide trout pond, halfway up a mountain. Especially halfway up a mountain in New England.

Eric stared at the dolphin for a while, wondering how it could have got there. And then the dolphin poked its head out of the water and stared back. Finally, it leaned against a rock and spoke. . . .

Other Apple paperbacks
you will enjoy:

The Bears Upstairs
by Dorothy Haas

Vicki and the Black Horse
by Sam Savitt

Kavik the Wolf Dog
by Walt Morey

Hi Fella
by Era Zistel

Swimmer
by Harriet May Savitz

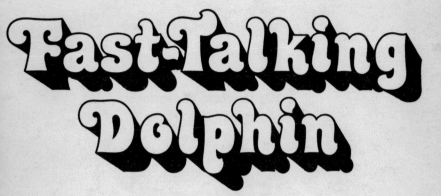

Fast-Talking Dolphin

Carson Davidson

Pictures by Sylvia Stone

AN
APPLE
PAPERBACK

SCHOLASTIC INC.
New York Toronto London Auckland Sydney

For Mickie

More than yesterday ...
less than tomorrow

ISBN 0-590-42513-7

12 11 10 9 8 7 6 5 4 3 2 1   6   9/8 0 1 2 3 4/9

Printed in the U.S.A.

Eric was surprised when he saw the dolphin. He'd never seen one before, but all the same he knew what dolphins were. He also knew where you found them, and this was definitely not where.

Not in a ten-foot-wide trout pond, halfway up a mountain. Especially halfway up a mountain in New England.

Eric stared at the dolphin for a while, wondering how it could have got there. And then the dolphin poked its head out of the water and stared back. Finally it leaned against a rock and spoke.

"I'm informed that your species
  Is gifted with speech,
But you've less to say
  Than a clam on the beach;

Pray, why don't you talk?
  Are you just not inclined?
Or must I assume
  That you're weak in the mind?"

Eric gulped. He'd heard that dolphins were pretty smart. But not *that* smart. Before he could figure out what to say, the dolphin spoke again.

"A bit backward, I see —
  Yes, the brain slightly lame,
But can't you say *something*?
  Perhaps state your name?"

"My name's Eric Anderson," said Eric. "Do, uh — well . . . do dolphins have names too?"

The dolphin peered at him somewhat coldly.

"What, me? Go about
    With no name? That's absurd!
I am Wallingford Ullingham
    Lowell, the Third.

    "However," he said, "you may address
me as Wallingford if you like."

    "Oh," replied Eric. "Well, uh . . . could
I just call you Wally?"

    "Certainly not." Wallingford's tone of
voice left no doubt about it at all.

    "Oh, sorry," Eric said quickly.

    "Quite all right.

"Your suggestion perhaps
    Was a trifle ill-bred,
But we'll simply consider
    The whole thing unsaid."

    Wallingford then sank into the water
and circled slowly around the pond. Was
that all? Eric wondered. Not even a good-
bye?

    But after a while the dolphin rose to the
surface again and gazed at Eric in a
fatherly sort of way. "Yes, yes, quite all
right. We'll consider it unsaid."

Eric looked around at the forest and the steep sides of the mountain. He couldn't help asking, "Wallingford, what're you doing in — well, that is, how'd you happen to get *here*?"

Wallingford leaned closer to Eric and whispered, "Gross and culpable malfeasance."

"Gross and *what*?!"

"Sloppy baggage handling," said Wallingford, translating graciously. "Some bumbling lout at the airport failed to lock the cargo door of the plane. So out I tumbled. In the middle — you might say — of nowhere."

"You fell out of an *airplane*?! Into *that* little pond?! Oh, come on!! Why, you'd have — "

"Ah, they'll miss me at the convention," Wallingford continued, taking no notice of Eric's last remark.

"A forest is fine,
    In its pastoral way,
But it just isn't London,
    Whatever you say."

"You were going to London?"

"I was, indeed I was.

"To a big oceanography
  Conference, you see;
I can't think what they'll do —
  They'll be lost without me."

Eric was pretty sure he didn't believe any of this. London, or conferences, or falling out of airplanes.

And yet . . . if it wasn't true, how *did* Wallingford get here? He certainly hadn't been in the pond before. Eric knew — he'd caught two trout in it last Tuesday. It was all quite confusing.

"Well, boy," said Wallingford cheerfully, "these things happen. Actually, this isn't such a bad place to be.

"I believe I'll stay on
  For a week or two more,
Provided it doesn't
  Turn into a bore."

Stay on?!! Just how did Wallingford think he could do anything else? He talked

as if he might slap on his hat and stroll
down the mountain almost any minute.

But maybe it would be better not to go into that right now. So Eric changed the subject. "Wallingford, do you always talk like that?"

"Like what?"

"Well — that way. Like a poem, or something."

"Ah, that," replied Wallingford.

"Well, I sometimes indulge,
    And I sometimes desist,
But a well-chosen verse
    I find hard to resist.

The most casual thought
    Can become quite majestic,
When properly rhymed
    In the best anapestic."

"In the best ana — *what*?!"
The dolphin eyed Eric soberly.

"It grieves me to find
    That it's as I suspected —
Your classical schooling's
    Been sadly neglected."

He pointed a flipper at Eric. "Anapestic is a type of verse. A poetic form. It is much favored by the more serious-minded poets — amongst whom, I believe I may say, I am numbered."

"Oh, I'm sure you are," said Eric hastily. He certainly didn't want to offend the only dolphin he'd ever met in his life. Especially a dolphin in a trout pond halfway up a mountain.

"What did you say that was? Antiseptic?" Eric wanted to get the word right. It seemed to be important somehow.

"No — anapestic. The most distinguished dolphins always speak anapestic."

A stray thought had been lurching around in the back of Eric's head for some time. Now he finally got hold of it and pulled it out. "Wallingford, dolphins are salt-water animals, aren't they . . . I mean, aren't you?"

"Salt-water?" Wallingford said vaguely. "I suppose so. Yes, I daresay we are. Why?"

"Well, here you are in fresh water.

There's no salt in this pond at all. Isn't that dangerous?"

"Oh, water's water," the dolphin said with an airy wave of his flipper. "What's a little salt?"

"Well, I think it's — "

"Don't give it a thought," Wallingford told him firmly. "Will power is the thing. That's what counts. If there's anything to this fresh-water business, will power will overcome it. Just a matter of letting every-one know who's boss."

"Well . . ."

"Will power," Wallingford announced again. The discussion was closed.

Eric looked at his watch. Oh, great! He was half an hour late for dinner already. And it would take another twenty minutes to get down the mountain. "Look, Walling-ford, I have to be going. But — is there any-thing I can do for you?"

"Do? For me? Of course not. However, you might come by and visit sometime if you like," Wallingford told him.

"I'm not partial to people —
    They talk all the time;
What they say is a bore,
    And they can't even rhyme.

But you — well, you're tolerably
    Silent, I've found,
And I don't think I'd mind
    If you care to come round."

Eric had turned to go when Wallingford
added, "No others, though — definitely no
others." He waved once and slid back into
the water.

The next morning Eric woke up worrying. Was Wallingford right? Could dolphins live just as well in fresh water? Did he really know, or was he just guessing?

I've got to get into town, Eric thought. I've got to look it up—find out once and for all. Right now, before it's too late.

He looked over at his brother Karl, who was still asleep. He wanted to tell Karl about Wallingford. He wanted to tell his mother and father too. But Wallingford had said no others. Definitely no others.

Eric got dressed quietly. Then he headed down the big creaking stairway. The stairway had creaked ever since he could remember, and his father said it had creaked ever since *he* could remember.

It was an old house. Old, and rambling, and painted bright yellow — like everything else in sight. Pig pens included. His father liked yellow. He said the way business conditions were going for the small farmer, at least the buildings ought to look cheerful.

Because of the yellow paint, the house didn't seem very old. But Eric knew it had been built in 1766. He'd been up in the attic, and seen the hand-hewn wooden beams. They were held together without nails — just wooden pegs. And he'd read the old records telling why the house had been put up in the first place.

It was before there was any farming in the valley. But there was a road — the old Post Road to the north. This house used to be an inn for travelers.

It was an important stop in those days. It was marked on the old maps, just like a town. Ransom Vale, it was called. The place was still Ransomvale Farm, but it wasn't on the road maps anymore.

Eric's father was just coming in from the barn. He and the hired hand had been out milking, same as they did every morning in the week. Every morning in the year, for that matter. Up at 4:30 — in for breakfast by 8:00.

"Good morning!" said his father. "How's the gentleman farmer today?"

His father called him and Karl gentleman farmers because they didn't have to get up in the morning. But he said they had a right to sleep while they could. Soon enough they'd have to stop being gentlemen and start being farmers.

"Hi, Dad," Eric said. "How was milking?"

"Fascinating. Absolutely fascinating. Something new every minute. Right now I'm training the spotted Guernsey to give green milk."

"Green? Oh, come on, Dad!"

"I figure it'll be great for making pistachio ice cream. Well, I'm happy to say she's pretty much got the hang of it already. This morning she produced a batch that any true Irishman would be proud to see. As I say, endless excitement down in the barn."

His father liked to talk that way sometimes.

Breakfast was terrible. His mother was usually the best cook in the township, but when she got upset things went downhill in a hurry. This morning, it was clear to everyone at the table that she was *very* upset.

"All right, what is it?" his father asked finally.

"It's that man Benson! He shot at little Allen Watkins yesterday."

"Did he hit him?"

Eric's mother banged a pot onto the stove. "No. They say he fired over Allen's head, just to scare him. Same as he did with the Smith boy."

She plunked down a big bowl of oatmeal on the table. "I don't care where he fired. Something's got to be done about that man! Sooner or later he'll kill someone's child!"

"I know," said Eric's father soberly. "I've talked to the sheriff — couple of times. He just keeps saying that after all the kids were trespassing."

"Trespassing! No sane man shoots at a trespasser!"

"I told the sheriff that too. He mumbled something about looking up the law one of these days."

Eric's mother turned suddenly to the two boys. "You two — you keep away from that Benson! *Way* away! His house, his barn — anything. Don't even go down that road. I mean it! That man . . . that man's crazy!!"

Eric already had a pretty good idea of that. Only he wouldn't have called old man Benson crazy — he'd have called him *mean*. Mean clear through. Especially when it came to kids.

His mother smiled at the two boys. "Sorry I shouted that way. It's just that I worry about you, with somebody like that on the loose."

Eric wasn't as worried as she was. He

never went near Benson's place anyway. He'd decided a long time ago that it was better to stay away from *him*.

But Eric wasn't really thinking about Benson. He was thinking he had to get to town. He had to find out if Wallingford was right — if he really was safe in fresh water.

After breakfast Eric went round to the tool shed and got out his bicycle. He was about to set off when his father stopped him. "Feel like doing a little fencing today, Eric?"

"Well, I sort of wanted to go down to —"

"Good, I knew you'd give me a hand. We've got to fix up the east pasture — lost another heifer out of there yesterday."

Eric groaned to himself. The east pasture was the biggest one on the farm. It would take days. "Gee, Dad, could I just go into town first and —"

"Fine. I'm glad you're going to help. Let's amble on up there before we lose any more stock. Go get the small tractor, will you?"

And so it was settled. They went up into the east pasture with the tractor and a wagon full of fence posts and barbed wire. Eric drove. Whenever he and his father went out with a tractor, he always drove. He liked it, and he did it well.

His father had been driving tractors for a good long time now, and he was pretty well bored with the whole thing. Besides, Eric seemed to *understand* tractors. He thought on their wave-length. He could usually tell when one of them was about to break down, and why.

The fences in the east pasture were in pretty sad shape. No wonder the heifer had got through. The wonder was that any were still there.

Eric and his father set to work. Wherever a post was beginning to go, they'd stop and put in a new one. Then they'd stretch the barbed wire, pulling it up as tight as a violin string. It was nasty stuff to work with, and a hot day to do it on.

About mid-morning they stopped to rest. They had a drink from the spring at the far side of the meadow. Then they sat down under the trees and did nothing at all for a while. At last Eric turned to his father and said, "Dad, what do you know about dolphins?"

"Dolphins? Well, not much. They've been tried, but they're not a good cash crop for this kind of land."

Eric sighed. "No, I mean it, Dad. Do you know anything about them really?"

"Why? You thinking of bringing one home? I guess you could keep it in that empty stall at the end of the barn."

"Please, Dad." Eric was getting a little desperate. "I just want to find out if it hurts a dolphin to live in fresh water. Do you know?"

"Fresh water? No, son, I don't. But it sounds pretty important to you. Why?"

"Oh, it's just — I was curious, that's all."

"That's all?"

"Sure, Dad."

"Okay, if you say so. But you can have that empty stall any time you want."

Eric was hoping he could go up to see

Wallingford that night after work. But by the time they'd quit fencing, and driven the tractor back down, and had dinner — it was just too late. It was even later the next night.

The job took them two and a half days. Right after lunch the day they finished, Eric set off down the township road on his bike. The state highway was faster and not so dusty, but it was full of cars.

Eric didn't like cars. They took up too much of the highway to suit him. That was the great thing about the township road — no cars. They were always in too big a hurry.

When he got into town he headed straight for the library, and when he got into the library he headed straight for "Dolphins." There wasn't much there that was any use to him. Eric had a scientific sort of mind, and he wanted a book that was as serious about the subject as he was. As it turned out, there was only one.

The first thing he learned from it was that dolphins came in quite a few different

types. Wallingford, it seemed, was a bottle-nosed dolphin. He didn't think Wallingford knew that, and he tried for a moment to imagine what his friend's reaction to it would be.

Bottle-nosed. Somehow it didn't sound very dignified. Eric decided that particular bit of news would be a very good thing not to tell Wallingford.

Next Eric read that dolphins were high-speed swimmers — faster than most ships. Interesting, but not much use in a ten-foot pond. He learned that dolphins could find things in the dark by bouncing sound waves off them — just like the Navy's sonar. Again, no great help up in that pond.

But finally . . . yes! Here it was. Dolphins, the book said, could manage in fresh water for a short time. But before long they would begin to sicken. In the end, death would result.

Eric shut the book with a slam. He was immediately stared at by a lady who was reading a cookbook, and glared at by the librarian, who was doing a crossword puzzle. But he never noticed — he was thinking about the water problem.

That silly dolphin! He didn't even know he was in trouble! He could talk anteptic or whatever it was — he did that just fine. But he couldn't tell when he was in the wrong kind of water.

He needed a keeper, that's what he needed. And suddenly Eric realized — he was it.

Eric decided that the fact book might come in handy. Who could tell what other problems would come up, now that he was a dolphin-keeper? So he carried it over to the librarian to be checked out.

She looked at Eric. She looked at the book. Then she looked back at Eric. "Are you sure you want *this* book?" she asked. "I really think it might be just a bit . . . well, grown up for you."

"Thank you, but I—"

"Now, if you're interested in dolphins, here's something I'm sure you'd like better. It's got a real story in it, and it has lots of pictures."

"Thank you very much," said Eric politely. "But I think I'd rather have this one."

"Well, if that's really what you want." She stamped the book, and Eric took it out and tossed it in his bike basket. Then he pedaled home.

"Hi!" said his mother, giving him a quick kiss on top of the head. "Where'd you go loping off to?"

"Library." He held up the book.

"Dolphins, eh? Well, when you find out all about them, tell me, will you? I think they're cute."

"I don't know about cute, but they're pretty smart. That much I know already."

"Oh, I believe it," his mother said. "Tell me, how'd you like to grab a tractor and drive me up in the far woodlot? I want to get blackberries for a couple of pies."

Usually Eric would have jumped at the chance. Partly because of the pies, partly just for the fun of driving the tractor. But today he had more important business.

"I'd love to, but . . . well, there's something else I've got to do. Is it okay? I mean —I really have to."

"Really have to, eh? But not about to tell me what it is. All right, you go do it. I'll walk—it's probably better for me anyway."

Eric headed straight up the mountain. He was determined to have it out with Wallingford. He was going to tell that fast-talking dolphin exactly how much danger he was in, and they were going to make a plan. Now.

But as soon as he got to the pond Eric forgot all that. Wallingford was lying half out of the water, gasping and moaning. His eyes were shut—badly swollen. His mouth was hanging half open. He was struggling desperately to breathe.

"Wallingford!" Eric shouted. "What's wrong?"

The dolphin opened one eye and looked up at Eric. "Slightly indisposed," he said thickly. "Nothing to be concerned about. A little will power, and I'll soon be right."

"You're dying! We've got to *do* something!"

"Dying? Nonsense. Nothing of the sort. Merely a — " Wallingford fell to coughing.

"It's the fresh water, Wallingford! It's killing you! We've got to get you into salt water — fast!"

Wallingford looked up at him. "Fresh water? No, no, nothing to do with it. Just a somewhat suspect fish I ate. I thought it looked a touch scruffy, but — " He fell forward, gasping. He couldn't raise his head.

Eric didn't wait to see any more. He was already racing down the mountain. He had to get back into town before the stores closed. He had to get salt! He had to! If he didn't make it, Wallingford would be dead before morning.

This time he took the state highway instead of the township road. He didn't care about cars. The highway was faster. That was all that mattered now.

He made it to the hardware store by three minutes past five. The shade was already down. The door was locked. But Eric beat on it wildly, and Mr. Hudson finally came and opened it.

"Well, well, *well* now, young Eric
—what's all the fuss? This isn't the emer-
gency ward, you know."

Eric was so winded he couldn't say anything at all.

"All right, all right, just come on in and
catch your breath. I reckon you must have
something on your mind, from the look of
you."

Finally Eric managed to gasp, "Salt.
Need . . . bag of salt."

Mr. Hudson looked puzzled. "Salt? Why not go to the grocery? They've got salt."

"Don't understand. Need . . . *lot* of salt. Big bag."

"Oh, rock salt. But that's for melting snow. Why on earth do you — oh, never mind. Don't try to tell me. You just wait here."

Eric nodded, still puffing. He wasn't going anywhere. Not without the salt.

It took Mr. Hudson quite a while to find the stuff. But finally he came clumping down the old wooden stairs with a burlap bag in his arms and dropped it heavily on the counter. Rock salt. It weighed more and cost more than Eric had any idea it would. It took almost all the money he had.

Getting the bag home on the back of his bike was no picnic. But getting it up the mountain just about finished him. It took him an hour and three-quarters, including rest stops. Also including twice that he dropped the bag and it almost split.

Eric didn't go straight to the trout pond.

Instead he circled carefully around it.
Once he peeked through the trees and saw
Wallingford still lying across the rock.
There was no sign of life. But then Eric
heard a faint gasping and coughing.
Maybe there was still a chance.

He worked his way back to the creek.
He was just above the waterfall that
splashed into Wallingford's pond. He
poured a good big dose of salt into the
water and watched as it swirled down-

stream, disappearing over the waterfall.

As an afterthought Eric threw in another couple of handfuls. No use doing it half-way.

But that salt wouldn't last in Walling-ford's pond forever. And he couldn't stay here all night throwing in handfuls of the stuff. He needed a timed-release system.

Eric thought about that for a while. Then he took his bag of salt and poured a pile of it onto a rock in the middle of the stream. Every little while some water splashed up onto the rock, bringing down a bit of the salt with it. He figured that ought to keep a fairly steady level of it in the pond. At least for tonight.

Eric shoved the rest of the salt behind a boulder. Then he took a deep breath and set off for a walk in the woods. Maybe he ought to go down and stay with Walling-ford, but he just couldn't bear to see his friend like that. And he had done as much as he could. Now he could only wait.

Finally, he headed back toward the pond. If the salt was going to work at all, there ought to be some change by now. As he got closer, Eric felt his heart beating wildly. Would Wallingford be any better, or would he be . . . dead?

Eric needn't have worried. When he got to the pond, Wallingford was splashing around at high speed, chasing a trout. Having finished that, he looked up. "Ah, there you are, boy."

"Feeling better, Wallingford?" Eric sat down on a rock.

"Better?" The dolphin was plainly puzzled.

"I'm as fit as a good
  Stradivarius fiddle;
But why do you ask?
  Is this some sort of riddle?"

Eric began to feel unreal. "But . . . but don't you remember?"

"Remember? Remember what?"

"Well — well, how sick you were. Wallingford! It was just a few minutes ago!"

"Sick?" said Wallingford lightly. "Absurd! Must have been somebody else.

"I've no use for a doctor,
   A drug, or a pill,
For I've simply refused
   All my life to be ill;

I put up with no nonsense
   Or grief from a germ;
It knows who's the boss
   If you always stand firm."

Eric was beginning to wonder if he'd been dreaming. Could he have imagined the whole thing? Could Wallingford not have been sick at all? What was real?

But then Eric saw a long wet spot on the rock. The spot where Wallingford had been lying — half-dead — not long ago. And Eric knew it had all happened just as he remembered it.

Poor Wallingford. He just couldn't admit he'd been so sick. He couldn't admit how much he'd needed help. That was it. Wallingford couldn't admit he *needed* anyone or anything.

But he did. And somehow that made him seem much more . . . more human.

Suddenly Eric was filled with a great feeling of warmth for his new dolphin friend. But all he said was, "Good night, Wallingford. I'll see you soon."

"Come back anytime. Always glad to see you, boy."

"My name's Eric," said Eric.

"Ah, is it? Well, good-bye now."

That night Eric couldn't fall asleep. He just kept thinking about his problem up the mountain. How was he going to keep that pond supplied? The salt-on-the-rock system would do for a while, but he'd have to go up the mountain two or three times a day to add more.

That was just too many times a day, however much he liked Wallingford. His family would begin to ask questions. And he couldn't answer them because Wallingford had said he had to keep it all a secret.

That was another thing. It was going to get harder and harder not to tell people. His mother was already looking at him a little strangely. His brother Karl just plain suspected something — no question about it. Karl was no dope. Sooner or later . . .

The next morning Eric set to work solving his first problem — salt supply. He collected some old odds and ends of lumber, and took them off to the tool shed. He spent the morning hammering and sawing and nailing.

His family was used to that. Eric was always inventing things. Sometimes they knew what he was making, and sometimes they didn't. This time they didn't. They spent a lot of time guessing, but they never got close.

Karl thought it must be some kind of crazy boat. Mostly because it had a paddlewheel at one end. That made more sense than anyone else's guess, but it still wasn't right.

Eric finished his invention that afternoon. He waited till no one was looking and took it off into the woods. It wasn't easy to carry. That paddlewheel seemed to get mixed up with every tree and bush he

passed. Getting the thing up the mountain
took him almost an hour.

He circled around Wallingford's pond
and went on up to the top of the waterfall.

All his salt had washed off the rock in the middle of the stream. Eric set up his invention on the rock, with its paddlewheel in the water. Then he poured the rest of his salt into the other end of it.

It went to work immediately. The stream turned the paddlewheel around slowly. The paddlewheel turned some gears and pulleys. The gears and pulleys worked on the salt supply, dropping a little of it into the water every couple of minutes. Just enough, Eric figured, to keep Wallingford's pond nicely salt-conditioned.

He sized up the amount of salt in the machine. Enough for three or four days, he thought. And then what was he going to do? He'd spent most of his money already.

Eric put that problem out of his mind. He'd solve it tomorrow, somehow or other. Meanwhile he went down to see how Wallingford was.

Bouncy was how Wallingford was. He'd invented a game which involved leaping out of the water and grabbing a leaf off a tree. In his teeth.

"It's not that I care for
   The flavor of leaves,
Since most of them taste
   Like a coal miner's sleeves;

It's really the sport
   Of the thing, don't you see;
Doesn't do to get flabby,
   I'm sure you'll agree."

Eric was worried about all this bouncing around. "But Wallingford, suppose you land wrong? If you hit one of those rocks you'd—"

"Land wrong?

"Any dolphin you choose
   Is an expert at this;
We've been leaping for centuries—
   How could we miss?"

"Well . . . "
"Note the third branch on that big white birch. See the missing leaf? That's my high mark so far. Now stand back."

He swam down to the bottom of his pond, getting up speed. Suddenly he shot skyward. There was a brief flash of Wallingford nibbling at the tree, and then a neat splash. When he came to the surface, he had a leaf in his teeth.

"Look at that. Good foot-and-a-half higher. Makes you proud to be a dolphin."

Eric couldn't help being impressed. It had been quite a jump. And Wallingford had kept his promise. He had come down in the exact center of the pond, nowhere near any of the rocks.

"That was great, Wallingford. It really was. My brother Karl would love to see you do that. Couldn't I . . . well, couldn't I bring him around some day?"

"Another boy? No, I think not. Don't like people particularly — they talk so much."

"You'd like Karl. He doesn't talk very —"

"Now you, boy — you're all right.

"I must say I've taken
    A liking to you;
You know how to listen,
    Which few people do.

For the most part they jabber
    And gabble like geese;
They ought to be jailed
    For disturbing the peace.

There are problems I'm solving
    That weigh on my mind,
And privacy's vital
    For things of that kind."

"But Wallingford, Karl wouldn't —"

"Privacy, boy. Most important thing in the world to a real thinker."

At this point Wallingford ended the conversation by making another leap up into the birch tree. "Higher again," he announced proudly. "At this rate I may get right to the top of it before night."

"Wallingford, about all this jumping in the air — couldn't you get your exercise just as well chasing fish?"

"Well, the fish situation's
   A bit of a bore;
I seldom see many
   Around any more.

There were squads of them here
   Just a few days ago,
And where they've all gone to
   Is more than I know.

Do you think they disliked me,
   Or felt I was rude?
They're so *touchy*, you know,
   If they're in the wrong mood."

He looked very puzzled about the whole

thing. But Eric didn't notice — he was thinking about this new problem. Good grief. Wallingford didn't even know what had happened to all the fish. That was like his brother Karl not knowing what had happened to all the candy bars.

"Well," said Wallingford sadly, "I'll have to give the matter some cogitation, I suppose."

"Cogi — what was that?"

"Some heavy thinking about. Pity, what with all the other important questions I have under consideration at the moment."

"But what good is heavy thinking? You've already eaten the — "

"When these little problems come up, you have to be firm with them, that's all. Not enough fish? Be firm. Weather too warm? Be firm."

Wallingford pointed a flipper at Eric. "If you insist that life measure up to the standards you set for it, you will seldom be disappointed. Accept no second-rate performances. It merely takes will power."

Eric started to say something, but decided against it. He didn't want to spend all his time arguing with Wallingford. Besides, what was the use? Wallingford knew how to do a lot of things, including talk. But there was one thing he didn't know how to do — listen.

So Wallingford continued to leap for leaves, and Eric sat on the bank, thinking glum thoughts. First it was salt — now it was fish. What was he going to do?

He'd solved the salt problem, sort of. But where was he going to find fish? Live fish? And how was he going to pay for them?

After a while Wallingford came down to earth and looked at Eric. Then he looked again, harder.

"You seem gloomy, my boy —
    Rather sad and withdrawn;
The good cheer that I usually
    See is quite gone.

Is it bad marks in school,
    Or a kite in a tree?
The state of the world,
    Or a broken TV?

Is it rabies? Or dandruff?
    A blighted romance?
Or mayhap your problem
    Is one of finance?"

Eric wasn't about to discuss the matter with him. That last guess had come much too close to the truth. So Eric decided to talk about something else. "That was a nice poem, Wallingford. Was it in antep —whatever that was?"

"Anapestic. Yes, I always use the anapestic form. It's so much more . . . more elegant. If you know what I mean."

"Oh, I do. It was very elegant." Eric stood up. "Well, good-bye, Wallingford. I've got to go."

"Good-bye, boy. Do come again tomorrow."

"I will. Oh, I'm sure I will," said Eric a little grimly.

He went down the mountain very confused about what was going to happen next.

What happened next was that Eric got a job. He didn't have much choice. It was either earn some money — or watch Wallingford slowly starve to death. Even now his dolphin friend was beginning to get a lean and hungry look that Eric didn't like at all.

The only choice was which job. And that turned out to be not much choice either. There was only one he could find where the boss would give him a week's pay in advance. That was important. He didn't think Wallingford could wait for a week. He looked as though he needed a square meal right now.

So Eric went to work for Mr. Hudson, at the hardware store. There was another good reason for that too. As an employee he got a much lower price on salt. He could see that he was going to need quite a lot of that, as time went on.

At first he felt pretty sorry for himself. Here he was working, while all his friends were swimming and playing baseball and biking. But then he remembered that he was doing it for Wallingford. Wallingford, waiting up there in that pool. Wondering where all the fish could have gone to.

Anyway, Eric liked it at the hardware store. He discovered he could do all sorts of work he'd never been hired for. Before long he knew where to find all the gizmos and mohaskas and thingamajigs, and what they were for when he'd found them. From then on he could wait on customers just as well as Mr. Hudson.

At first some of the customers objected. But they quickly found that Eric knew what he was talking about, and what *they* were talking about. Most of them came to prefer Eric. He moved faster.

At one point Eric was in the back room weighing up ten-penny nails. As he finished, Mr. Hudson came in and saw him. "Oh, by the way, something I should have told you before. You know Mr. Benson?"

"Well, sure."

"If he comes in for ammunition, don't sell him any."

Eric stared at him. "You mean just tell him he can't buy it?"

"Right. That man's dangerous. Mighty dangerous. He's going to kill somebody sooner or later, probably a child. I don't want him to do it with my ammo."

"He'll only get it someplace else."

"I know that. I can't do a job the sheriff ought to be doing. But at least I can stop him from getting the stuff here. So no ammo."

Mr. Benson didn't come in, though. Doesn't need any more ammunition, Eric thought to himself. Probably has enough already to wipe out half the township.

After his first day's work Eric helped

Mr. Hudson lock up the store. Then he went out looking for fish.

He found that storekeepers tended to look at him very strangely. "Live fish, sonny? No, we never carry 'em. Who'd want live fish? You can't cook 'em till they quit wiggling."

But Eric figured they had to be alive and wiggling, or Wallingford would know there was something wrong. As Eric's father might have put it — something fishy.

Eric got the same answer the second place he tried, but this man had an idea. "Look, go over and see Mr. Goldberg. Seems to me he's got a customer — a restaurant or something — that uses them. You try Goldberg. If anybody's got live fish, he does."

Mr. Goldberg did indeed have them. "It's that tourist restaurant out by the lake. They keep a tank of them, right by the front door."

"Why do they do that?"

"Customer comes in, points to a fish, says he wants that one. Then they cook it up for him. It's sort of a sales gimmick."

Anyway, Eric got his first batch of fish. He went off down the street with a pail of them in the front basket of his bike. He didn't know they were going to splash so much water around, and he didn't see why most of it had to catch him in the eye.

Mr. Goldberg watched him pedal away. "Now why," he asked himself, "does this boy want two dozen live fish when he hasn't got a restaurant? Why?"

Then he shrugged. "All in good time, Goldberg. When he wants to tell you, he'll tell you. Till then, whose business is it? Not yours."

Eric had begun to wish he were hauling salt again. Salt was heavier, but it didn't jump. Every one of his fish seemed to be trying for a world record. And they weren't like Wallingford. They didn't bother to plan a landing till it was too late.

So every minute or two Eric had to stop and rescue a fish. At first they landed in the road. Then on the way up the mountain they landed in bushes and behind

rocks. One of them even made it into the stream and got away completely.

But finally he got the twenty-three fish up to his salt machine. Now what? Should he throw them all in at once? Or try to do it little by little, like the salt? Eric decided to toss in the whole pailful. He figured they'd wash over the waterfall a few at a time, so Wallingford wouldn't be able to eat all twenty-three at one meal.

Then Eric went down for a chat. He found the dolphin drifting around on his back, eyes half-closed.

"Sleepy, Wallingford?" Eric asked.

"Ah, boy, there you are," he replied cheerily. "No, I was not reposing, but composing. I have a little poetic work in progress — an ode to the sky. It goes like this:

"Oh, cloud-spangled sky,
    So majestic, so vast,
As glorious now
    As in centuries past,

Oh, how happy your life!
    Oh, what joy comes to you!
And yet, sky, how often
    You seem to look blue.

Oh, glorious sky,
    Become bold and triumphant!
Cast off this sad color and . . ."

Wallingford ground to a halt.

"What's the matter?" asked Eric.

"I've painted myself into a corner. Nothing rhymes with 'triumphant.'"

"Nothing?" Eric thought about it for a while. "I guess you're right," he said finally. "Nothing does."

"Pity. It was going so nicely too. Well, no use crying over it. There'll be other odes along tomorrow."

Just then Eric saw one of his twenty-three hand-carried fish come washing over the waterfall. He decided not to point it out. Let Wallingford find his own grub. It would be character-building for him.

"Yes, yes," Wallingford continued, "there'll be other odes along tomorrow. Odes are easy. For those of us who have the gift, that is."

"Gift? Can't all dolphins do it?"

"Gadzooks, what an idea! No, most of them are as stupid as . . . well, as people. But we anapestic dolphins are quite different. For us, composing an ode is a snap.

"The various verse forms
    Are our cup of tea;
It's the logical way
    That our minds work, you see.

We can dash off a sonnet
   Without any warning
As simply as most folks
   Can wish you 'good morning.' "

"I've noticed. It's great!"

Wallingford beamed. "Thank you, my boy. We're the cream, you might say — we anapestics."

"Wallingford, what does that word mean exactly?"

"Anapestic? Well, it's a kind of verse with an accent every third syllable. There's also iambic, of course — with an accent every second syllable. Very poor stuff."

"Do any dolphins speak that — the iambic?"

"A few, I think. Somewhere or other. But your average dolphin isn't even up to that. He can only speak prose."

Wallingford leaned against some rocks and pointed a flipper at Eric, just like the teacher at school. "Prose, my boy, is a form of spoken or written expression in which the rhythmic pattern tends perceptibly toward the random, as opposed to the more uniform and codified systems of syllabification."

Eric stared at him. "Wallingford, that was the most complicated explanation of a perfectly simple word that I ever heard in my life."

Wallingford looked offended. "And how, pray, would *you* define it?"

"Prose is the way people talk all the time."

"Oh." Wallingford considered that for a while. "Well, yes, I suppose you could put it that way."

"You could if you wanted anyone to understand you," Eric said. "Anyway, these other dolphins speak prose. Doesn't it make them feel kind of left out when you talk antep — when you talk poetry to them?"

"Oh, we don't mix with them socially. It's been tried, but it just doesn't work out. For us *or* for them. They're always happier when they stay with their own sort."

Eric had a feeling he'd heard something like that somewhere before, but he let it go. "Wallingford, you remember I told you about my brother Karl? Well, would it be all right now if he came up and—"

"Oh, no, no, no. I told you before—no visitors. I've got all sorts of difficult questions under consideration. Privacy vital. Quite vital."

Just then Wallingford spotted the new fish in the pond, and gave chase. A moment later he returned, looking happier.

"You notice that the fish are starting to come back already. Will power, you see. It never misses. Remember that, boy—it'll be useful to you later on. Life won't always be as easy and carefree as it is now. Someday you'll have to face problems. Someday you'll have to go out and earn a living, not only for yourself but for others. Then you remember what I've just told you. You'll thank me for it some day."

Eric didn't say anything. He was fond of Wallingford, very fond of him. But there were times . . .

And so the summer wore on. Eric worked every day at the hardware store, learning more and more about gizmos and mohaskas and thingamajigs. Every so often he struggled up the mountain with salt. Every so often he struggled up with live fish. Wallingford wasn't exactly getting fat — but he wasn't starving, either.

Eric discovered that he was becoming the township expert on dolphins, poetry, will power, and several more of Wallingford's favorite subjects. Not to mention hardware. All in all, things were going as well as he could expect.

By this time Mr. Goldberg was used to seeing him come in for more fish. They would usually talk a bit — the weather, what was wrong with Mr. Goldberg's fish freezer, how the home team was doing. Things like that. But Mr. Goldberg never asked about the fish and what Eric might be doing with them.

After a while Eric began to feel a little embarrassed about it. Finally he said one day, "I suppose you're wondering why I keep buying all these fish."

"Wondering, yes. Asking, no. If you don't want to talk about it, don't talk."

"Well, I . . . I guess I'd rather not, Mr. Goldberg."

The man patted Eric's shoulder and gave him a kindly smile. "So don't. It's a basic constitutional right, to keep your mouth shut."

"Thank you."

"Don't thank me. Better men than I am wrote up those rights for you. Me, I just approve of the job they did, and try to learn by their example."

Eric had been doing his best to hide the heavy traffic in salt and fish that was passing through the farm and up the mountain. His father didn't notice because he was always in the barn or out in the fields. Karl did, though. He started asking questions that Eric found harder and harder to answer.

His mother noticed too. She didn't say anything for quite a while. But finally one day she stopped him and asked what was going on.

Eric had been afraid all along that this would happen. He still didn't know what to say. But his mother was standing there with that no-nonsense look on her face, and he had to tell her something. "I . . . well, I need this stuff to help a friend."

His mother waited, but Eric didn't say any more. Finally she broke the silence. "Salt? And live fish? What kind of friend is this?"

Eric felt awful. He'd never had secrets from his mother and father. But he couldn't tell on Wallingford. He just couldn't. "Please," he begged, "can I not tell you? Not for a little while. Please."

His mother looked at him very hard. "Eric, are you doing something dishonest?"

"Oh, no! Really — no!"

"You promise me?"

"I promise."

She thought about it for a minute. "All right, you take your salt and your fish, and you help your friend. I hope he appreciates all this, whoever he may be."

"Well, no, that's not quite his style."

"Not his style to say thank you, eh? Would it be prying if I were to ask what *is* his style?"

"Anapestic, actually," said Eric. Then he thought to himself, Hey! I've finally learned to pronounce it.

His mother looked at him rather strangely, but she didn't say anything more.

The first thing Eric saw when he got near the trout pond was a spout of water. Eric figured Wallingford must be behind it, somehow or other.

Actually, he was under it. Directly under. He was shooting all this water into the
air through his blow-hole. He looked quite
proud.

"Well, whales can blow geysers,
    So why shouldn't we?
All the books say they're in
    The same family, you see.

They rumble and grumble
　　And try to deny it,
But a whale's just a dolphin
　　In need of a diet."

"But most dolphins don't blow like that,
do they? It must have been pretty hard to
learn."

"Will power, that's what did it."
Wallingford ducked under the water and
blew another geyser. Eric had to move fast
to keep from getting soaked.

"As a matter of fact," Wallingford went
on, "I'm pretty sure it's not talent on the
whales' part — just leaky plumbing. I don't
think they *want* to do it at all. They can't
help it. We're better constructed than they
are, so we don't leak to begin with."

Eric wondered if that was the whole
story. He'd have liked to hear the whales'
side of it.

Wallingford turned over and floated on
his back.

"You'll note that my water spout's
　　Higher and wetter,

For anything whales can do
    We can do better."

Eric decided not to comment on that. Instead he asked, "How's the fish supply holding up these days?"

"Adequate. They haven't all come back, but I make do, I make do. Seems to me they're smaller than they used to be, though."

Eric had hoped Wallingford wouldn't notice that. Mr. Goldberg was trying to get bigger fish for him, but he just couldn't find any.

"Oh, I forgot to tell you," said Wallingford. "Something most annoying happened yesterday. *Most* annoying. There was a boy around here."

"There was?! *Who?!!*"

Wallingford shrugged off-handedly. "He didn't say.

"In fact, he said practically
    Nothing at all;
He seemed a bit stupid,
    From what I recall.

You'd have thought from the pop-eyed
    Expression he wore
That he'd never seen dolphins
    Around here before."

Oh, great! thought Eric. Now they were *really* in trouble. Big trouble. In this township, when one kid knew, every kid knew. There'd be mobs up here like the seventh game of a World Series.

Unless . . . unless it was his brother Karl who'd come by. Eric knew he could trust Karl not to talk. He hadn't told Karl about Wallingford, of course — not after everything Wallingford had said. Still, he could trust Karl.

"Look, this is important. Was . . . " But Wallingford wasn't listening. He was eyeing a leaf in one of the trees above his head.

"Wallingford!" Eric shouted. The dolphin looked down. "This is important! Was he a kind of dark-haired kid with — "

"Oh, no — very light-haired. Blond, actually."

That did it. It wasn't Karl. And whoever it was, he'd tell every kid he could find before he even stopped running.

There was one more thing Eric had to find out. "Tell me, did you . . . " But Wallingford was eyeing the leaf again.

"*Wallingford!* Did you . . . did you talk, when he was around?"

"When who was around?" asked Wallingford vaguely.

It wasn't easy, but Eric kept his voice quiet. "The kid. The boy who came by here yesterday. Did you talk ·when he was around?"

"Well, not very much,
   For he wasn't too bright,
But one has to say *something*;
   It's only polite."

"Oh, good grief! He heard you talk!"

"Well, I imagine he did, unless he was stone deaf," said Wallingford.

Eric went home very gloomy. Whoever he was, this boy knew there was a dolphin in the trout pond. He knew the dolphin could talk. That really did it. By tomorrow every kid in the township would be up there, with friends from the next county.

So much for Wallingford's privacy. Privacy! He'd get more of it in a goldfish bowl on the Courthouse lawn. Eric could see it all now. The place would be like a circus. Great. Just great.

So how was he going to deal with *this* one?

Eric woke up early the next morning. It was light outside, but not very. The sun was just coming up.

He couldn't see it—his room was on the west side of the house. But he could make out the first rays touching the weather vane on top of the barn. Like everything else around, the weather vane was yellow. Except where the rising sun began to turn it a soft red.

Eric heard his father start down the stairway. Creak—creak—creak. He waited for the loud one, the fifth. Creak—*creak!* Then two more normals, and a real screamer. Creak—creak—CREAK!!

Every now and again his father talked about fixing those stairs. But somehow the fences always seemed to need it more, so everyone just listened to the creak. Then they went back to sleep again.

Eric was in no mood to sleep this morning. He was thinking about that kid, whoever he was. This was the biggest problem yet, and he couldn't handle it alone. It didn't matter any more what Wallingford wanted or didn't want. Eric had to tell someone else — he had to have some help.

He went over to Karl's bed and began shaking him.

"Huh? . . . what?" Karl mumbled. "What's wrong?"

"Shhh. I have to tell you something. Right now!"

A few minutes later they were out in the corn patch, where nobody could hear them. "A *dolphin*?" Karl was saying. "Up there?! Oh, come on — dolphins live in the *ocean*! Florida, California — places like that. Probably what you saw is a — "

"Karl, will you for once just shut up and listen? I know a dolphin when I see one, and this is a dolphin. His name is Wallingford. He told me that he was — "

"*Told* you?!"

"Yes, told me. He speaks better English than you and I put together. Now, please — just pipe down and listen. I've got a big problem, and I need help."

He told Karl all about Wallingford — the salt, the live fish, the poems he made up, the leaping he did to grab leaves — everything. As he went on, Eric could see that

Karl was slowly beginning to believe him.

Finally, Eric told him about the kid who had come up and seen Wallingford. "The trouble is, I don't know who he's talked to. So we've got to do some detective work. We've got to find out how many kids already know about Wallingford."

Right after breakfast Eric and Karl set off down the road on their bikes, going in opposite directions. Luckily it was haying time, and the hardware business was slow. Mr. Hudson had told him not to come in for a few days.

Within half a mile, Eric came to the Sanders place. There was no one in the house. He went out to the barn. Empty. He looked in the milk house and both silos.

Also empty. He could tell where Mr. Sanders was from the sound of the tractor, but no one else was around.

Finally he spotted Keith and Charlie up on a hill beyond the main pasture. They were kite fighting. They had broken glass or razor blades or something like that glued to their kite strings up near the top. Keith was trying to cut Charlie's string — and Charlie was trying to cut his.

Nobody knew why the Sanders boys had taken up kite fighting, but they spent most of their time at it. A couple of other kids had tried it that summer. The trouble was, Keith and Charlie had got so good that no one else had a chance against them.

So there they were, at it again. The kites

were swooping and diving, looking almost alive. Keith and Charlie were doing a lot of fancy foot-work and arm-waving, so they didn't see Eric till he was almost there.

"Hi, you guys!" said Eric.

Charlie looked down from his kite. "Hey, Eric! Haven't seen you in weeks. How's the hardware store?"

"It's okay," Eric answered. "I kind of like it. And the money's not bad either."

"Good. I'll know where to come when I want to borrow some. Hey, watch this!" Charlie suddenly raced around his brother, swinging his arm in wild half-circles.

His kite ducked down under Keith's. Then it bobbed up on the other side, climbing straight up. The two kite strings almost touched. But at the last second Keith lunged backward, and his kite sailed up and over Charlie's.

"Almost got you!" said Charlie.

"You did not! I saw you coming a mile away. I could have got *you* if I'd wanted to."

"Okay, okay," Eric said, "you both looked pretty good."

The boys stopped their fight and sat down to rest. Eric picked a long stem of meadow grass and began to chew on it.

Trying to sound casual, he asked, "What's been happening? — besides kite fighting, I mean."

"Oh, you know, not much. Couple of calves born this week."

"Pa's not going to keep either of them, though," Keith added. "He says they don't look stupid enough to be good milkers."

Eric chewed on the stem of grass some more. "That's all?"

"Oh, yeah — we were down to the County Fair the other day. It's not very good this year."

Eric looked at the two brothers suspiciously. "*Nothing* else going on?"

"No, not much that — oh, I forgot! We found something out in the woods yesterday!"

Eric sat up suddenly, his heart pounding.

"Or was it yesterday?" Charlie stopped

and looked at Keith.

"Was it?" Keith scratched his head. "Well, let me see. Day before yesterday we went swimming, and the day before that we . . . what did we do?"

The Sanders had a reputation for talking everything into the ground. Right now Eric thought they might talk him straight into the insane asylum.

But finally Charlie said, "Yeah, sure — it was yesterday. I remember because the second calf was born in the morning. Anyway, what we found was a whole pile of old sugar buckets up by Castleton Ledge!"

"Sugar buckets!" Eric exploded.

"Yeah! I didn't know anybody ever sugared up in there. But we looked around and sure enough — there was a whole grove of maples. Big old trees. Eighty, ninety years old maybe."

"That was all? You didn't see anything else?"

"Well, we tried to find the sugaring shed, but it wasn't there. Maybe they brought the sap down and boiled it around here someplace."

Sugar buckets, Eric thought as he rode off. That's their earthshaking news — maple sugar buckets.

But he got the same sort of red-hot information at the next place he stopped, and the next. A broken bicycle. A trip to town. A picnic. Stuff like that.

Finally Eric sat down on a rock to think it over. It just didn't make any sense. Are these kids holding out on me? he asked himself. Have they somehow figured out about me and Wallingford, and just decided not to talk?

Well, there was only one thing to do. Call their bluff. It meant taking a chance, but he had to do it.

The next one he talked to was Fred Applegate, and Eric didn't waste any time. "Hey, Fred, did you hear about the dolphin?"

"Oh, come on, don't give me that. Everybody's seen that old dolphin."

Eric's heart sank. He almost groaned out loud. "Everybody?"

"Big deal dolphin. So he swims around, and he jumps out of the water, and he eats a fish. So what? I got better things to do than watch that all day."

Poor Wallingford. How he must hate all this. Kids staring at him, shouting at him, probably poking him with sticks. Eric felt awful. Why hadn't he been able to stop this? He'd failed. He'd failed when Wallingford needed him most.

Eric stared miserably at Fred. "Were there a lot of kids up there?"

"Well, everybody that had the money, I guess."

"Money!! You mean someone's charging *admission*?!!"

"Sure. What'd you expect?"

"Well, I didn't think they'd—"

"Who needed that mangy old dolphin? If I hadn't blown all that money there, I could have taken another ride on the roller coaster."

Roller coast—oh, good grief! The County Fair! There must be a dolphin down there in the sideshows.

8

Eric spent the rest of the day hearing about the dolphin at the County Fair. It seemed to be a pretty boring animal. No talent, no personality, no nothing. Clearly a prose type, thought Eric.

And that night after he got home Karl gave him the same report. When you mentioned dolphin to any boy or girl in the township, you only heard one story — I want my money back.

"All right," said Eric, "nobody knows anything. That much we're sure of. This guy hasn't opened his mouth."

"Not yet," said Karl glumly.

"Yeah, but it's crazy. What kid do you know would wait around with news like that?"

"Well . . . none, I guess."

"Right—none," said Eric. "But all the same, there is one. Why isn't he talking?"

"Maybe he hasn't got anybody to talk to."

Eric was about to say something, but he stopped with his mouth open.

Then he replied slowly, "Smart, Karl. Very smart. Maybe he just hasn't got anybody to talk to. All right, who do we know that—"

And then they both said together, "Herbert Benson!"

Herbert! The kid with no friends. Everyone knew why Herbert didn't have any friends—it was his father. Mr. Benson, the guy with the gun. The guy who shot at kids.

Eric called him mean—a lot of people called him crazy. Mr. Benson didn't like anyone. Most of all he didn't like kids. He wouldn't let Herbert play with anybody, ever. No one knew whether Herbert minded that or not, but he did what he was told. He was the kid with no friends.

And then Eric remembered something

else. "A blond kid! Wallingford said this kid was very blond."

"Herbert."

"Sure, it's Herbert. Can't be anybody else."

They both sat there and thought for a while. Then Karl said, "There's one person Herbert could tell."

"That's what I've been thinking," said Eric grimly. "He could tell his father."

Suddenly Eric sprang up. "I've got to get into town. Tell the folks I may be late for dinner."

"They won't like that."

"I know," said Eric as he swung onto his bike.

He didn't even bother to go to the Courthouse — he knew it would be closed. Instead he went straight to Mr. Pearson's house.

Mr. Pearson was the Town Clerk. He came to the door on Eric's third ring, looking sleepy. As Eric talked, though, he began to wake up. "You want to get into the town files? *Now?*"

"Please, Mr. Pearson. It's awfully important."

"I guess it is, if you rode all this way just to do it." He scratched his chin. "Well, I sure don't feel like going down there myself. But I'll tell you what I'll do, Eric. I'll give you the key to the place."

"Oh, thank you, Mr. Pearson! I really appreciate that."

"You've got to promise me you won't go into anything else. Just the town files. And have the key back here inside of an hour."

"I promise, Mr. Pearson."

"All right, then. Off you go."

Eric knew right where to look. It didn't take him very long to find what he was after — Mr. Benson's property deed. One look at that, and he knew that his suspicion had been right. Wallingford's pond was on Old Man Benson's land.

Eric was late for dinner, all right. Usually his mother and father would have had a good deal to say about that, but he was looking so unhappy that they didn't have the heart. His mother didn't even ask where he'd been. She just took him out to the kitchen and heated up some leftovers for him. Eric hardly knew what he was eating, though. He was too busy worrying.

The meanest man in the township. Far and away the meanest! And Wallingford had to be on *his* land!

By the next morning, Eric had made up his mind. He had to talk with Herbert, no matter how risky it was. He climbed on his bike and went up to the Benson place.

He hung around just out of sight, waiting for his chance. An hour crept by. Then two. Several times he caught sight of Herbert doing chores around the farm yard. Once or twice he thought Herbert was headed his way. But he always stopped.

By the middle of the afternoon Eric felt

half-starved. But he wouldn't give up. Not if he had to sit here till the moon came up. It was too important.

And finally he got his chance. Herbert walked up into the wood lot with an axe on his shoulder. Eric circled around the back way to cut him off without being seen from the house.

He found Herbert felling firewood. "Look, I've got to talk to you."

Herbert jumped and whirled around. "Eric! Hey, you better get out of here. If my father sees you, he'll — "

"I know what he'll do. I don't care — I've got to talk to you."

"Me? Why me?"

"Herbert, you saw Wallingf — you saw a dolphin up the mountain, didn't you?"

Herbert looked at him, his eyes wide with surprise. "How'd you know that?"

"Never mind. I know." Eric took a step closer. "Herbert, did you tell your father?"

"I . . . well, not at first. But finally I did, yes. This afternoon."

"What did he say?"

Herbert looked away. He shifted his feet a little. He started to say something — then stopped. He spent quite a while scratching his arm. He started to speak again, and caught himself.

Finally Eric repeated, "What did your father say, Herbert?"

"He said . . . he said he's going up there tomorrow and shoot it."

Eric got up very, very early the next morning. Even his father was still asleep. He woke Karl, and together they slipped quietly out of the house. Without a word, they set off in opposite directions.

A few hours later, Mr. Benson also left his house and headed up the mountain. There was a heavy rifle over his shoulder. Herbert plodded along beside him, looking up unhappily at the rifle from time to time. At last Herbert spoke.

"Sir?"

"Well?"

"Do you . . . do you have to shoot it?"

"No, I don't have to shoot it. I *want* to shoot it."

"Yes, but—"

"The animal's on my property." Mr. Benson's voice rose. "My property! I'll do with it as I see fit. And I'd like to see any of these busybodies around here try to interfere."

"Sir, couldn't you just—"

"Now look, Herbert. That animal's got meat on it, just like any other animal. Meat costs money. That's what's important—not some stupid feeling you got about the animal."

"Sir, this isn't an ordinary—"

"That's enough, Herbert."

"But this dolphin is different! It can—"

Herbert saw his father's eyes narrow. "Yes, sir," he said miserably.

But when Mr. Benson got to the trout pond, he found some unexpected company. A circle of Eric's and Karl's friends stood around the pond, their arms locked. They watched quietly as Mr. Benson came through the trees. None of them moved.

"All right, you kids," Benson shouted, "clear off my land! You're trespassing!"

Eric looked at the rifle and swallowed. "No, Mr. Benson." His voice shook a little, but he kept on talking. "Your land isn't legally posted. We have as much right here as you do."

"What d'you mean, not posted? You saw that sign down there, didn't you?"

"I saw the sign, Mr. Benson. It's no good. To be legally posted, you have to put up a notice every 400 feet all the way around your property line. And date each one of them every twelve months."

Benson took a step forward. "Oh, so you're one of those kids, eh? A legal big-mouth. Okay, since you're such an expert on the law, I guess you know that you're blocking access to my pond. *That's* illegal."

"We know," said Eric quietly.

"Then clear out!"

"No."

Slowly Benson raised his rifle and point-ed it at the silent circle gathered around the pond.

"Now get!" he roared.

For several seconds the circle held. Then one of the boys cut and ran. The others closed up the gap and stood waiting, watching Benson.

And then Herbert Benson left his father's side. He walked slowly forward until he stood facing Eric. Everybody else stared at him — not knowing what he was doing. But Eric understood. He dropped his grip on Karl's arm, and Herbert slipped into the circle beside him. Locking arms with Eric and Karl, he stood facing his father.

Benson lowered his rifle. His voice was very quiet. "Herbert, come here."

There was a short silence. Then Herbert said, "No."

"No, what?"

"No, sir."

"You know what's going to happen to you when I get you home."

"Yes, sir."

"All right, stay there if you like. Now listen to this, all of you. This silly stunt of yours doesn't interest me in the least. I came here to do a job and I'm going to do it. So get out of my way, or you'll pay for it."

Benson started forward. The group stood, not moving. The man stopped in front of Eric. "I said, *get out of my way!!*"

For a few seconds everyone remained frozen. Then Benson lunged at Eric with the butt of his rifle. The blow caught Eric in the shoulder and sent him spinning to the ground. He saw Benson raising the rifle. It was pointed at the pond.

Eric screamed, "Wallingford, get *down!!*"

There was a sudden thrashing of water as Wallingford dived. Benson pulled the trigger. And at the same instant Karl leaped forward and gave the gun barrel a shove. The shot went wild.

Benson turned on Karl. His face was twisted with fury. "Why, you dirty little —"

He swung the rifle up, over his head. Everyone there knew that one blow from the heavy wooden stock would crush Karl's skull like an egg.

Then it happened. It seemed almost like

slow motion, almost like a dream. As Benson swung at Karl, he stepped on a patch of wet moss. For a moment his foot held. Then it slipped.

He threw his hands into the air, trying to catch his balance. The rifle went spinning off into the bushes. For one long instant Benson teetered on the edge of the water. Then he fell.

His head struck the rock ledge beside the pond. Slowly he rolled over and sank into the water. A soft red swirl of blood showed where he had gone down.

Everyone was stunned — unable to move. But not Wallingford. In an instant he was flashing down, down into the depths of the pond.

And then — nothing. Eric expected him to rise again in a few seconds, pushing Benson to the surface. But time passed. And more time. Wallingford didn't appear.

What had happened? Eric peered into the dark water, straining to make out what was going on down there.

Then he looked up. There was something

else that had to be done. "He'll need a doctor. Somebody's got to go for one."

He glanced around. It had to be someone he could trust completely. Karl. But he'd need Karl for first aid. Herbert? No, he was probably pretty shaky by now.

Eric looked at Shirley Newson. Shirley was faster on her feet than most boys. "Will you do it?"

"Sure!" Shirley left on a run. Then everyone turned back to the pond. *What was taking so long?*

At last Wallingford burst to the surface. "Stick!" he gasped. "Need a stick . . . good and heavy!"

As the rest of them went running off into the woods, Eric asked, "What's wrong? Why's it taking so long?"

"Leg caught," said Wallingford. "Got jammed between rocks. Don't know how, but it did."

From up above the waterfall, Karl shouted down, "Is this big enough?"

Wallingford looked up. "Yes! Don't bring it — throw it!"

Karl's pitch was high. Wallingford leaped out of the water and caught the stick in midair. Then he dived to the bottom again.

Once more everyone waited. They could see a few brief flashes of Wallingford working with the stick, but that was all. There was no trace of Benson. After all this time it didn't seem possible he could still be alive.

Finally, Wallingford came up carrying Benson. Eric and Karl went to work instantly. Both of them had trained in life-saving techniques, and they knew exactly what to do.

But it seemed hopeless. Minute after minute went by, and nothing happened. No reaction. No sign of life. Nothing. They kept on, though — one working while the other rested.

Eric had just taken over again when the doctor arrived. "Keep on, Eric," he said. "Don't stop!" Eric kept on, and the doctor went to work beside him.

After a little while the doctor said, "He might be able to breathe by himself now. Let's try." Eric stopped working. Benson took a few ragged breaths, then nothing. "All right, Eric, back to it."

Finally the doctor said, "Let's try him again." This time Benson kept on breathing.

Some time later he opened his eyes and stirred. Then he tried to get up. "No, no," said the doctor. "You stay right where you are. You're a sick man yet."

"Sick? Sick?" Benson whispered hoarsely. "What . . . what's wrong? What happened?"

"You had a nasty accident. You just stay there and rest for a while."

"Accident? What accident? What are you —"

Then he looked up and saw the circle around him. "Kids. What do they — Oh! They were the ones! I remember it all. They did it!!"

"Take it easy, now," the doctor

cautioned. "Don't get yourself excited."

"Not get excited?! With them standing there? Those kids tried to kill me!!"

The doctor said very quietly, "Those kids, Mr. Benson, have just saved your life."

"They . . . they *what*?"

"They saved your life. They did the right things at the right time, and without them you would now be quite, quite dead."

"And Wallingford," one of the boys said. "Don't forget Wallingford!"

"Shhh!" Eric warned.

But it was too late. "Wallingford?" the doctor asked. "Who's that?"

Oh, well, Eric thought, I couldn't keep it secret much longer anyway. He said to the doctor, "The dolphin. Behind you, in the pond."

"A *dolphin*? Up *here*?! Eric, you're having some sort of dream. There aren't any – " Then the doctor turned and saw Wallingford. He didn't say anything at all, but his mouth kept on opening wider and wider.

"Wait a minute," said Benson. "Are you trying to tell me those kids . . . those kids saved me?"

"Yes," answered the doctor, pulling his attention away from Wallingford. "They did exactly that."

"I . . . I don't believe it! They just told you that!"

"They didn't tell me—I saw."

"They . . . they really did that?"

"I said that before, Mr. Benson. They did."

Then Eric spoke up. "It was more Wallingf—it was more the dolphin than us. He got you out of the water."

"The *dolphin*?!"

"Yes, Mr. Benson," said Eric. "Your leg was caught under a rock. He got you loose."

"The *dolphin* did that?"

"Yes. None of us could have."

Benson turned to Herbert. "Is this true, Herbert?"

"Yes, sir."

"That . . . that animal pulled me out of the water?"

"Yes, sir. You were down there a long time. He had to work awfully hard to get your leg unstuck."

Benson fell silent. The doctor did a few quick tests on him, and then said, "All right, Benson, I think you're ready to navigate. But take it slow. I'll have a couple of the kids help you down the mountain."

Benson burst out angrily, "I don't need any kids—I can walk by myself!" He got slowly to his feet and looked around. He took a deep breath, as if he knew it was going to hurt him to speak. Then, in a different, quieter voice, he said to Eric, "Your dolphin friend . . . well, you don't have to worry about him. I won't try to hurt him again."

He started down the trail, holding onto trees and rocks as he went. Presently he stopped and turned around. This time it seemed to be even harder for him to speak. He looked at them all for a moment and then said slowly, "You kids . . . thanks."

When he had gone, Eric asked Herbert Benson, "Does he mean that — about not hurting Wallingford? Can we really trust him?"

"Oh, yes. My father's a hard man, but when he says he won't do something, he won't do it."

10

Next day Eric and Karl and their friends went to visit Wallingford. They walked up the trail talking and laughing — all except Eric. He was a hundred yards behind, thinking.

Thinking about Wallingford, of course. He was thinking about all the crowds that would be stamping up this trail soon. After yesterday, there'd be no way to keep it secret. Everybody'd be up here.

Everybody in the township — everybody in the county. Half the state, probably. And reporters, to spread the news for anyone who might have missed it. In other words, a mess.

He would handle it somehow, of course — he'd handled the salt problem, and the fish problem, and the Benson problem — but he wasn't looking forward to it. It was going to be a mess, no question about it. A fifteen-round World Championship mess.

Up ahead of him Eric could hear the others talking. Keith was telling Herbert Benson about kite fighting. Of course.

"It's great, Herbie! It really is! Hey, how'd you like to come around tomorrow and try it?"

"Sure — only I haven't got a kite."

"No problem. We'll lend you one. How about it?"

"Okay, great! I'll be over right after chores."

Eric couldn't help smiling. Herbert Benson had stopped being a kid with no friends.

When they got to Wallingford's pond, he immediately went into his famous birch-tree act. He leaped higher than ever before,

right up into the top branches of the tree.

"Stupid dolphin at the fair sure couldn't do that," said Fred Applegate. "And this doesn't even cost anything."

At last Wallingford stopped jumping and settled down for a while. There was a loud round of applause. Wallingford bowed grandly, looking very pleased with himself. He had clearly changed his mind about how much privacy he needed.

Eric asked, "You working on anything new these days, Wallingford?"

"As a matter of fact, I am," Wallingford replied. "You see, I've always wanted to be a real expert at something. Not just a state expert, or even a U.S. expert, but a *world* expert."

"World expert at *what*?"

"Well, I gave that quite a lot of thought.

"There are all sorts of experts
    On all sorts of things,
There are experts on cabbages,
    Experts on kings.

There are experts on roosters
    And roofers and rookies.
And writing the fortunes
    Inside Chinese cookies.

Experts on coaxing
    The ice into cubes,
And coaxing the toothpaste
    Inside of the tubes.

But since none of these fields
    Was quite my sort of dish,
I became the world expert
    On how to call fish."

There was a puzzled sort of silence. Finally Eric said, "How to call fish? You mean like Joe or Mabel?"

"No, no. Not how to name them. How to call them. Some people do hog calling — I do fish calling. Listen to this."

Wallingford reared back and delivered a long, high-pitched whistle. "That's to get their attention. Now comes the message."

What followed was the strangest assortment of noises Eric had ever heard —

clicks, squeaks, grunts, clacks, and yelps. It all lasted about ten seconds, and it worked like a shot of TNT. Three fish came squirting over the waterfall immediately. Wallingford leaped up and got them in midair, all three in one mouthful.

"World expert," said Wallingford with a modest smile. Almost everybody applauded wildly. The only one who didn't was Eric — he just sat there, stunned.

That did it. That really did it. Now that Wallingford had learned this handy-dandy little trick, he could clean out half a week's supply of fish at one meal. It would take a night-and-day bucket brigade to keep up with him. How was Eric going to cope with *this* one?

But Wallingford wasn't finished. "Next I thought I might try flying. It looks like great fun, and it ought to be pretty easy."

Eric stared at him. "Flying?! Easy?!"

"Oh, yes. I've been studying a few birds I happen to know, and it looks like a snap. Has to be, if they can handle it. What with *their* seven-watt intellectual equipment."

Everyone laughed. "Birds aren't so bright, huh?" asked Betty Windham.

"Bright? Ha!

"I met one last summer,
   A wren or a jay,
Who, after much thought,
   Said, 'Nice weather today.'

Well, this witty remark
   Put such strain on his brain
That he suffered for weeks
   From a cranial sprain.''

They laughed again. But Eric was still thinking about that flying business. "Wait a minute, Wallingford. Did you really say flying would be easy?"

"Oh, rather," replied Wallingford lightly. "If you can leap, you can fly. Same principle, only more so."

Eric took a deep breath. He had a good deal he wanted to say about *that* idea. It was one of the craziest things he'd ever heard. Did Wallingford have any idea how much he *weighed*? Was he equipped with anything that looked to him like *wings*? Did he . . .

But Eric never got around to saying any of that. Because suddenly he stopped and asked himself — why did he want to argue about it? Why?

The plain fact was that life was more interesting Wallingford's way. Crazy or not, it was interesting. Eric was practical — he had enough of that for both of them. Practicality worked, but it was no real fun. Thinking you could fly was lots more fun, whether or not you ever did it.

Eric looked at Wallingford. That crazy dolphin! Suddenly he was overwhelmed with a great feeling of warmth. Then — without even thinking — Eric began to speak.

"It's great to be clever,
  And read all the books;
It's also quite nice
  To have health and good looks.

It's fine to have plenty
  Of money to spend,

But it's much more important —
To have a real friend."

For a moment there was complete silence. Wallingford looked at him with a strange expression on his face. Finally he said, "That was . . . that was very good, Eric. *Very* good."

At that moment Eric realized that something altogether new had happened. Not just that he'd said a poem in anapestic. Or even that Wallingford had liked it. No, something more important than that.

For the first time, Wallingford had called him by his real name. Wallingford had called him Eric. For the very first time.

But Wallingford was going on. "Very good indeed. I think perhaps . . . yes, I think it's time I made you one of us."

Eric stared at him blankly. "One of us?"

"Yes. I ought to speak with some of the others, I suppose. But just between ourselves, it'll be all right."

"What? What'll be all right?"

"Yes, yes, it'll be all right," said Wallingford. "Tell me, Eric, how would you like to become an honorary anapestic dolphin?"

For a moment Eric didn't quite know what to say. Then he looked at his friend and smiled, "I'd like that, Wallingford. I'd like that very much."

Later, when the others had gone, Wallingford said in a quiet, very serious voice, "I want you to remember, Eric, we will see each other again."

"See each other again? Well, of course we will — I'll be up tomorrow morning."

"No doubt, no doubt. But just remember what I said — we will see each other again, sooner or later." And then he smiled. Eric didn't know dolphins could do that, because they looked as though they were smiling all the time anyhow. But Wallingford smiled at him, and touched him once with a flipper. Then he dived down to the bottom of his pond.

Eric went to sleep that night worrying about the fish problem, and then woke up in the morning and worried about it some more. Three fish in one mouthful! And then three more, any time Wallingford felt like making that ungodly set of noises. How could anyone keep up with that?

Even if he had every kid in the township hauling buckets, and even if he could afford to buy all those fish in the first place . . . it simply couldn't be done. He'd just have to explain the situation to Wallingford, that was all. Tell him where the fish were coming from, and ask him to go easy on them. Ask him to give up fish calling. It wouldn't be easy — that wasn't the sort of thing Wallingford liked to hear at all. But he'd have to.

Anyhow, the first problem today was salt. His working supply up in the stream was getting pretty low. He was about to set off toward the mountain when his father stopped him and said, "We have to do some manure spreading today, son. I'll need you."

Eric knew it must be pretty important, because usually his father asked him, instead of telling him. And he figured his salt supply would hold out for a while yet. The fish would be gone, of course, what with that little fish-calling stunt, but a bit of dieting wouldn't hurt Wallingford any. It might even make him more reasonable about his future menu.

So Eric said, "Sure, Dad. I'll go hook up the spreader."

Manure spreading. Or, as his father sometimes put it, Perfuming the Great Outdoors. Everybody else on the farm

hated it, but Eric really didn't mind. It was certainly better than fence building. Almost anything was better than that.

They didn't talk much as they worked, partly because there was no sense in breathing any more than they had to. Of course, his father knew all about Wallingford by now, but he didn't mention the subject, and Eric didn't either.

The job took two days, and by the end of the second day Eric was really worried about Wallingford's salt supply. They finished Perfuming just before suppertime. As soon as supper was over Eric headed out the door with a flashlight in his hand. It wasn't dark yet, but he knew it would be before he got back. Then he changed his mind and got a kerosene lantern instead. In the end, a lantern was more reliable.

He lugged a bag of salt up the mountain and poured it into his machine. It was getting dark now. Picking his way carefully through the forest, he went down for a chat with his friend. A little chat about fish sources, and what happened when you took more out of a pond than was coming into it. Practical stuff like that.

There was no sign of Wallingford, though — he must be doing some heavy thinking, down at the bottom of his pool. He did that sometimes. Eric knew about how long Wallingford could stay under before he had to come up for air, and he sat down to wait.

Five minutes later he was beginning to worry. After six minutes he knew something was wrong. Six minutes was close to Wallingford's limit.

Could he be sick? Or . . . dead?

Eric lighted his lantern and peered down into the pond. By day it was almost impossible to see all the way to the bottom. But he found that if he held the lantern just right, the water turned crystal clear. And . . . and *Wallingford wasn't there!*

What had happened? Where could he be? Could he have washed downstream, into another pool? Eric went racing along the bank of the creek, straining to see to the bottom of every deep spot. Nothing. Not a shadow. He tried the other direction, upstream. Again, nothing. *Where could he be?*

Back at Wallingford's ex-pond, Eric sat down on a rock to think. And suddenly he remembered what that crazy dolphin had said yesterday, about learning to fly. Could he have? *Could he?* . . . Oh, that was ridiculous! No dolphin in the history of the world had ever gone flying.

Wallingford might be able to reel off anapestic poetry, but that didn't make him practical. He couldn't practical his way out of a wet paper bag. How could he fly clean out of a trout pond in the middle of New England? Answer: he couldn't.

But one thing was certain — Wallingford wasn't there. However he'd gone, he *had* gone. Eric would never see him again. No more crazy poems, or crazy jumping up into trees — no more crazy fish calling, for that matter. Just an empty pond in the middle of the mountains.

Suddenly Eric felt very sad, sadder than he'd ever been before in his life. He had lost a real friend, and he was going to miss him. He was going to miss that pest of an anapestic dolphin a lot.

Then Eric looked up, into the trees above his head. There in the flickering yellow light he saw something — a broken branch on Wallingford's favorite birch tree. How could that have happened? *How?* Did that mean that Wallingford really *had* . . . Oh, it was impossible! Dolphins just couldn't do that, not even Wallingford.

And yet . . . and yet, if he didn't fly, how *did* he leave? Eric shook his head hopelessly. There was no way of finding out, no way at all. He would never —

And then Eric realized. Benson!

Of course! Benson had broken his promise! He'd shot Wallingford, and then cut up the body and carried it out. Why not? He'd had two days to do it in.

And after everything Wallingford had done for him! Without Wallingford that man would be dead. And this was how Benson repaid him — by killing him!

A cold fury swept over Eric. Benson wasn't going to get away with this, not if Eric had anything to say about it! He'd go straight to the sheriff. Benson belonged in jail, and Eric was going to see to it that he landed there. It was the least he could do for his dead friend.

Then he noticed a tiny point of light through the trees. Someone was on the trail, carrying another lantern. Who could be coming up here at this time of night? Who would want to —

Benson! It must be! He must have figured out that Eric would be here, and was coming up to —

Eric left his lantern on the rock and got out of sight, fast. He crouched behind a boulder, trying not to breathe. He could hear the man approaching, making more noise than

people do when they're used to walk-ing in the woods. Then he realized that Benson would be looking for him in a few moments. He felt around on the ground till he found a good-sized stone. It wasn't much to defend him-self with, but it was something.

He was straightening up with the stone in his hand when a voice said, "Eric?" And it wasn't Benson at all! It was his father!

He dropped the stone and sauntered out from behind the boulder, trying to look as though he'd just been out for a short stroll in the woods.

"Hello, son," his father said, sitting down on a rock.

"Hi, Dad. What . . . what're you doing up here?" Eric sat down beside him.

His father looked at him silently for a moment. Then he said, "Well, I thought I owed you an explanation. So I've come to give it."

"Explanation? Of what?"

"Of why your friend Wallingford isn't here."

Eric stared at him, his mouth open. "Wallingford! You *know*?! But — but how did you — "

"A professor came by the other day, son. It was while you and your friends were up here."

"A professor? He came to the farm?"

"Yes. He'd just flown in. He's from a big scientific committee out in California, and he told us that Wallingford was supposed to be with them. He's been missing from their ocean research project."

"Oh," said Eric. "Oh, I see." He thought about that for a while. "But how did he know Wallingford was here?"

"You're more famous than you think, son. The doctor who was up here tending Benson — he spread the word in a hurry. After that, some of the news services picked it up."

"Yes, I was afraid they would," Eric said glumly.

"Anyway, the professor told me a couple of his people would come out from California to get Wallingford. They planned to hire a helicopter around here somewhere."

"A helicopter. Oh, that's how they did it."

"Yes. I pointed out that there was no place to land, but he said they didn't need to. Said they'd stay above the trees and pull him up in a sling."

Eric nodded. "The broken branch. No wonder it was—"

Then he stopped, suddenly realizing. "But you kept me down there spreading manure! You knew this was going to happen, and you kept me there!"

"Yes, son, I did. I didn't want you to—"

"You did it on purpose! You didn't want me to say good-bye to him! You let him just . . . go off, and I'll never see him again. And I never even said good-bye!" He made a choking sound — half-way between fury and tears.

"That's not fair! It's just not *fair*! He was my *friend*!!" Eric looked away from his father and stared angrily at the empty pool beside him.

"I'm sorry, Eric," his father said, putting a hand on his shoulder. "Maybe I was wrong to do that. I never claimed to be the smartest man in the county, but I did what I thought was best."

"But *why*? Why not even let me say good-bye to him?"

"Eric, I . . . I realized how you felt about Wallingford. I thought . . . well, I sort of thought you'd rather remember him the way he was — here in his pond, swimming around — instead of being cranked out on the end of a cable."

For a few moments Eric stared at the empty pool without saying anything. At last his father looked down at him. "Was I wrong?"

Still staring at the pool, Eric said, "I guess I . . . just hadn't thought about it that way."

He looked up at his father. "You're right, Dad. I would like to remember him like that — swimming around in his pond, about to jump for a leaf or make up a poem."

"There was something else," his father said, smiling a little. "I didn't think your friend would want you to see him leave like that. They tell me a helicopter lift isn't uncomfortable, but it isn't very . . . well, very dignified, either."

Eric had to smile too. "You're right about that. Wallingford wouldn't have liked it a bit." He looked up at his father again. "Thanks, Dad."

"I do my humble best," said his father, standing up. "Well, I'll be getting on down the mountain. I imagine you'd like to stay here a while longer."

"I guess I would, yes. And thanks for coming to tell me."

"My pleasure. Good night, Eric."

"Good night, Dad."

For a few minutes Eric just sat there, watching the lantern light flutter against the trees. He was thinking about his friend, and how much he was going to miss him.

After a while he began to wander aimlessly around the pond. As he got to the far side of it, something on the ground caught his eye. He bent over to look at it closer.

A message! It was a message scratched in the earth, so beautifully printed that it looked like a penmanship exercise. *Eric*, it read, *many thanks for all the salt and fish. And remember what I said the other day. Yours, W.* To one side was the stick it had been written with. Eric could see the toothmarks.

Thanks for the salt and fish. So that cagey old fraud had known all along! Smart, smart. But then there was that other part—*remember what I said the other day.* What was that? His wild talk about flying? No, Eric was sure that wasn't it. His opinions on the mental backwardness of birds? No, not likely either. And then Eric remembered.

"We will see each other again," Wallingford had told him, "sooner or later." It hadn't meant anything to Eric at the time, but now he understood. Suddenly he seemed much closer to his vanished friend. And suddenly he was sure that Wallingford was right—they would see each other again. Somehow.

Eric chose a very smooth, very round pebble and threw it carefully into the exact middle of Wallingford's pond. For luck. Then he picked up his lantern and headed down the mountain, toward home.